God Gave Us You

by Lisa Tawn Bergren · art by Laura J. Bryant

WaterBrook
PRESS

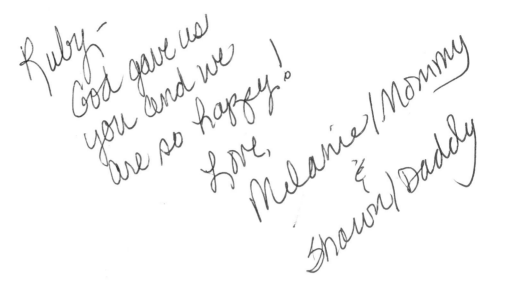

Ruby ~
God gave us
you and we
are so happy!
Love,
Melanie/Mommy
&
Shawn/Daddy

GOD GAVE US YOU
PUBLISHED BY WATERBROOK PRESS
2375 Telstar Drive, Suite 160
Colorado Springs, Colorado 80920
A division of Random House, Inc.

ISBN 1-57856-541-3

Copyright © 2000 by Lisa Tawn Bergren

Illustrations © 2000 by Laura J. Bryant

All rights reserved. No part of this book may be reproduced or transmitted in any form
or by any means, electronic or mechanical, including photocopying, recording, or by any
information storage and retrieval system, without permission in writing from the publisher.

WATERBROOK and its deer design logo are registered trademarks of WaterBrook Press,
a division of Random House, Inc.

Library of Congress Cataloging-in-Publication Data
Bergren, Lisa Tawn.
    God gave us you / by Lisa Tawn Bergren ; illustrated by Laura J. Bryant.—1st ed.
        p. cm.
    Summary: Mama polar bear tells Little Cub that her birth was a gift from God.
    ISBN 1-57856-323-2
    [1. Polar bears—Fiction. 2. Bears—Fiction. 3. Birth—Fiction. 4. Christian life—Fiction.]
    I. Bryant, Laura J., ill. II. Title.

PZ7.B452233 Go 2000
[E]—dc21   00-043245

Printed in the United States of America

2001

10 9 8 7 6 5 4 3 2 1

To Liv and Emma—

Words cannot express how glad
we are that God gave us you.
—L.T.B.

To Ron and Shirley—

Who have an endless supply of love and generosity.
—L.J.B.

"Good night, sweet child," Mama said
as she tucked Little Cub in.

But Little Cub wasn't quite ready to go to sleep.

"Mama, where did I come from?" she asked.

"From God," her mother answered. "Your papa and I were alone, and we wanted a baby."

"And you got me?" Little Cub asked, her voice muffled from under the covers.

"Yes, my special child. God gave us you."

"When we found out you were growing inside me,
we were so happy!
Even the angels were celebrating for us!"

"Because of me?" asked Little Cub.

"Yes, my darling child. Because God gave us you."

"And then what happened?" Little Cub asked.

"You started getting bigger and bigger and bigger,"
Mama said, kissing her. "And my tummy got bigger…"

"…and bigger…"

"…and BIGGER!"

"That was me inside of you?"
Little Cub asked in wonder.

"Yes, my special child. It was
you. God gave us you."

"Your papa talked to you and sang to you.
He wanted you to be born knowing his voice."

"Why?" Little Cub asked.

"Because he was excited. He was going to be a papa.
Because God gave us you."

"We went to the doctor and heard your heartbeat," she said. "I cried happy tears then."

"Why?" Little Cub asked. ("Why?" was Little Cub's favorite question.)

"Because God had given us you," Mama said.

"Every night, I prayed for
you, my special child. I prayed
that your bones would be straight
and your heart would be strong.
But most of all, I prayed that someday
you would love God."

"I love God," Little Cub said proudly.

"I know," said Mama. "I do too."

"And then I came?"
 Little Cub asked.

"Not yet," Mama answered.
 "We had to wait and wait and
wait," she said. "It seemed
 like forever. We got your
 nursery ready, and I
made up your crib.
 I even turned down the
sheet, so I could slip you
 right under the covers.
 But still, no baby."

"Did you wonder if God would ever give me to you?"
Little Cub asked. "On the outside, I mean?

Mama laughed. "I wondered.
But I knew you would come soon."

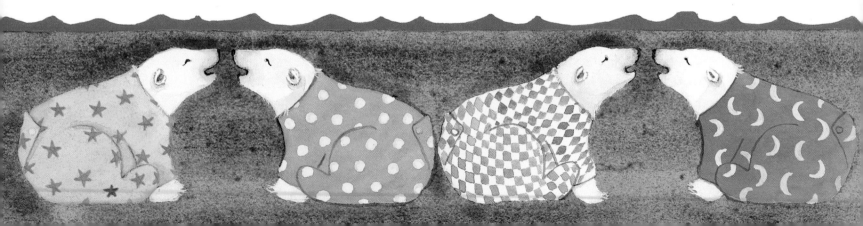

"And then what happened?"

"I felt something different. You wanted out!"

"I did?" Little Cub asked. "How did you know?"

"God gives mama bears special signals.
We raced to the hospital!"

"So then I was borned?" Little Cub asked.

"Yes!" Mama giggled. "And my, how you
        screamed and yelled. As much as we loved
meeting you for the first time, you missed
        being in my warm and cozy tummy."

Mama lowered her voice. "And then we took you home.
And it was just us. Our family. We just stared
and stared, wondering at the miracle of incredible you."

"Because why?"

"Because God had given us you."

"Umm, Mama? I was wondering…
Did you ever want a different baby? One like
Samuel the seal or Fredrika the fox?"

"Never," Mama said. "Never, ever, ever.
Your papa and I wouldn't trade you for the world."

"Why?" Little Cub asked.

"Why? Because God gave us you."

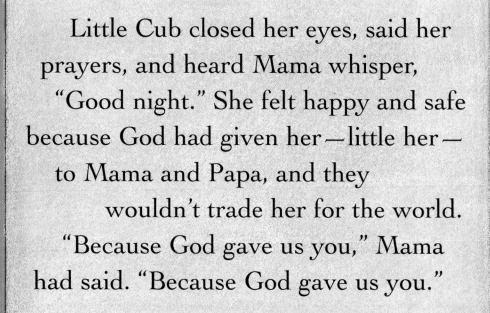

Little Cub closed her eyes, said her
prayers, and heard Mama whisper,
"Good night." She felt happy and safe
because God had given her—little her—
to Mama and Papa, and they
wouldn't trade her for the world.
"Because God gave us you," Mama
had said. "Because God gave us you."